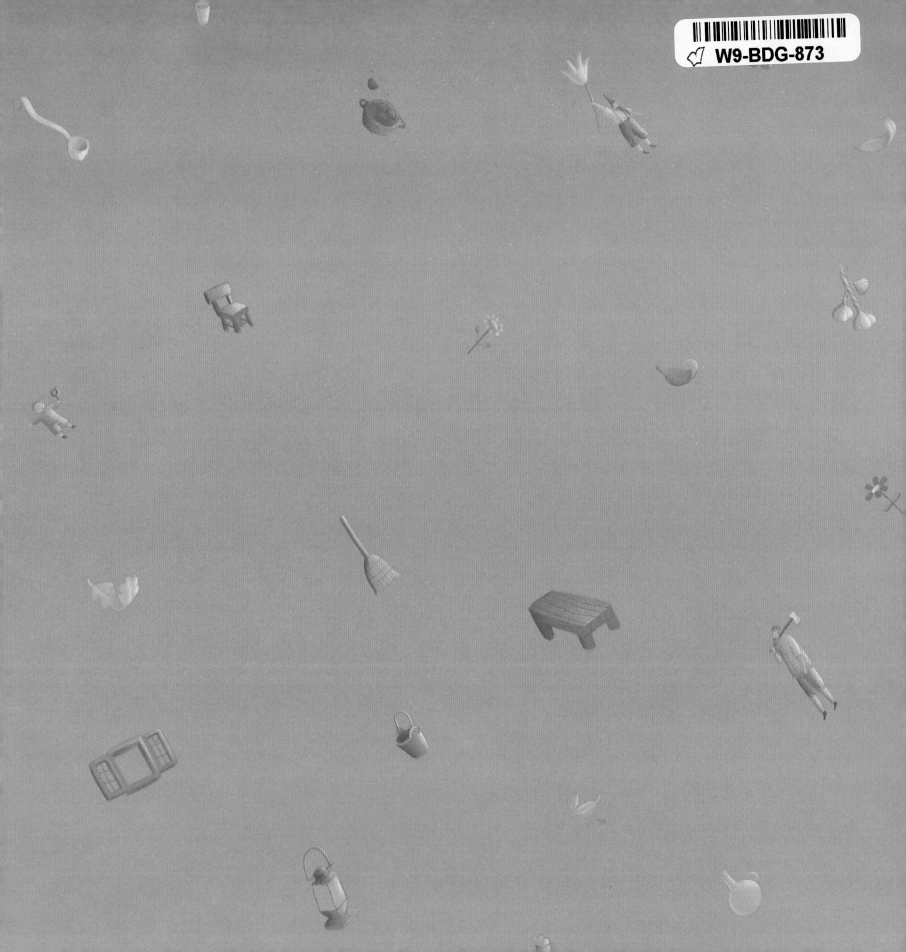

The Faerie's Gift

*The original seed of this tale was told to me by Eibhis De Barra
on the magical Isle of Cape Clear, off the coast of Southern Ireland.
A story of faerie ingenuity and human generosity, it can be
found in many forms across many cultures.*

Tanya Batt

For my Grandparents, whom I wish could be with me forever — T. R. B.
For my father — N. C.

Barefoot Books
3 Bow Street, 3rd Floor
Cambridge, MA 02138

Text copyright © 2003 by Tanya Robyn Batt
Illustrations copyright © 2003 by Nicoletta Ceccoli
The moral right of Tanya Robyn Batt to be identified as the author and
Nicoletta Ceccoli to be identified as the illustrator of this work has been asserted

First published in the United States of America in 2003 by Barefoot Books, Inc.

This book is printed on 100% acid-free paper
The illustrations were prepared in acrylics and oil pastels on Fabriano paper
Design by Jennie Hoare, England
Title lettering by Andrew van der Merwe, South Africa
Color separation by Bright Arts Singapore
Printed and bound in China by South China Printing Co. (1988) Ltd.

Hardcover ISBN 1 84148 998 0

1 3 5 7 9 8 6 4 2

Library of Congress Cataloging-in-Publication Data (U.S.)

Batt, Tanya Robyn.
    The faerie's gift / retold by Tanya Robyn Batt ; Nicoletta Ceccoli. —
1st ed.
[32] p. : col. ill. ;   cm.
Summary: One day, a woodcutter saves the life of a faerie from an attacking hawk, and
in return, is granted one wish. It seems like a wonderful gift, but when he listens to
needs of each one in his family, the gift soon becomes a burden. With thought, the
woodcutter figures out what the best wish will be.
ISBN 1-84148-998-0
 1 . Fairies Folklore. 2. Folklore. I. Ceccoli,
Nicoletta. II. Title.

398.221 2003

The Faerie's Gift

retold by Tanya Robyn Batt

illustrated by Nicoletta Ceccoli

Barefoot Books
Celebrating Art and Story

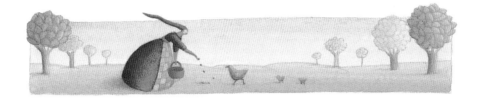

*O*nce upon a time, and it wasn't my time and it wasn't your time — it was a time when life was much simpler than it is today and magic was easier to find — in such a time there lived a woodcutter. He lived with his wife and his old mother and father in a small cottage on the edge of a forest.

Now the woodcutter and his wife had been married for a long time. More than anything else in the world they had wanted a child of their own. But the years had come and the years had passed, and never did the soft cries of a baby come to that house, or the sound of footsteps pittering and pattering on the stairs. And, if it wasn't bad enough never having what your heart desires, there was also the problem of the woodcutter's mother.

Once, she could see as well as you or I do, but as time passed her eyes grew dim and hazy, until finally, like a dark cloud moving across the sun, her eyesight was gone. Day in and day out she would sit, rocking in her chair beside the fire, the world about her like a curtain of darkness.

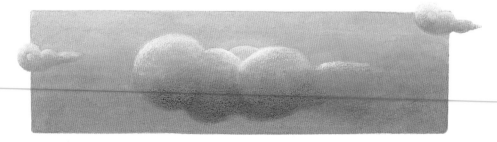

How the woodcutter wished that he had a child. And how he wished that his old mother could see again. He could have wept, but there was no time for tears. Life was hard. Old Man Poverty sat on the doorstep and snatched away everything good that came their way. The cupboards were often bare and their cottage was pricked by the bite of cold and the pinch of hunger.

Every day the woodcutter would swing his axe over his shoulder and head into the forest. There he would gather together bundles of wood to be sold at the market. It was hard and heavy work.

On one such day, the woodcutter stopped for a moment and rested upon his axe. He gazed up into the sky and there he saw a hawk circling above him. The hawk was hunting, and the woodcutter looked at the ground about him, trying to spy what it was that the hawk had sighted with its keen eye.

The woodcutter blinked in surprise. He could see a small man, dressed in ragged clothes, trying to hide under a fallen log. The man was hardly as tall as the woodcutter's hand was long. He was wearing a rough brown suit and was desperately trying to press himself between the ground and the log. It was a faerie!

The woodcutter remembered how his mother had talked kindly of the faeries when he was just a young boy. Without thinking, he stooped and picked up a stone and threw it toward the hawk. He didn't want to hurt the bird, just to scare it away from its prey. The hawk gave a cry and flew away.

The woodcutter turned back to the fallen log. The small man stepped from his hiding place and gave the woodcutter a nod.

"You have saved my life and for that I am most grateful. In return I'd like to give you the only thing I've got." The faerie man reached into his pocket and stepped forward. There, sitting snug in the palm of his outstretched hand, glowed a single wish.

"Take this gift and wish for what your heart desires," said the small man. The woodcutter carefully lifted the wish into his own calloused hand. It was the most beautiful thing he had ever seen. It seemed to dart and dance and sent a warm shiver through his body.

The woodcutter looked up to thank the faerie, but the small man had disappeared. He looked back at the wish he held gently in his hand.

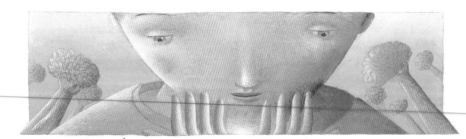

A wish. A wish! The woodcutter's heart gave a leap. He could wish for anything that he wanted. Suddenly he thought of all the things he had ever desired, all the places he longed to visit, all the fine food he would love to taste. And then the woodcutter thought of his family, sitting at home in the small cottage, cold and hungry. He knew that he couldn't keep that wish all for himself.

Quickly he turned and hurried home. He burst in through the door of the cottage and called his family together around the kitchen table. The story of the hawk, the faerie and the faerie's gift of a single wish tumbled from his mouth. He'd hardly finished his tale, when his wife gave a gasp.

"Husband, husband. Don't you see the faeries have given you that wish so that we might have a child? All these years of waiting and wanting, and now at last our wish will come true. Oh, it doesn't matter if it's a boy or a girl, so long as it's happy and healthy."

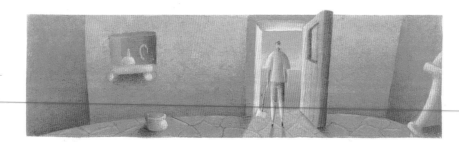

A baby. Suddenly the woodcutter felt ashamed of his own selfish thoughts. Why, of course, that's what they should wish for. What happiness a baby would bring to their lives. He was about to make the wish, when his mother said, "Son, son. It has been years since I saw the faerie folk, but they have not forgotten me. They know how it is with my eyes — how hardly a day passes without me wishing that I could look once again upon the green of the forest and the gold of the setting sun. Why, I can hardly remember what your own dear face looks like. Please, son, use your wish to give your mother back her sight."

His mother's sight. The woodcutter looked at the old woman sitting at the table. His own dear mother, who had nursed him as a baby and fed and clothed him as a child. He thought of all her kind words, her stories and her gentle touch. Surely he owed his mother this one kindness. And so he was about to speak the wish for his mother, when his father thumped a fist down upon the table.

"Son! Now you listen to me. Life is hard for us all. There is not a winter that passes that we don't near all starve and freeze to death. You've only the one wish and you must use it wisely. It's gold you should be wishing for. And lots of it. With gold we will be able to buy ourselves a happy and comfortable life."

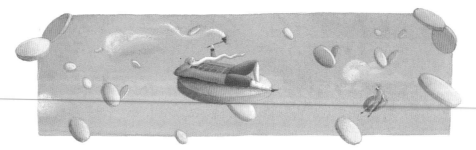

The woodcutter stared at his aged father. The old man hardly ever spoke. Now as the woodcutter listened to his father's words, they seemed strong and wise. If they had gold, their lives could be so different.

But the poor woodcutter had only the one wish. What should he choose? A baby for his wife and himself? Sight for his blind mother? Or gold as his father insisted? Suddenly, that one wonderful wish seemed to him to be nothing but a heavy burden. How could he know what was the right thing to wish for?

The woodcutter stood up and left the table. He went out of the cottage and began to walk. Through the forest he went, up the hill and across the fields. He walked the day to its end. The sun began to sink in the west and the night sky twinkled with a sprinkling of silver stars, and a fingernail of a moon hung against night's dark blanket.

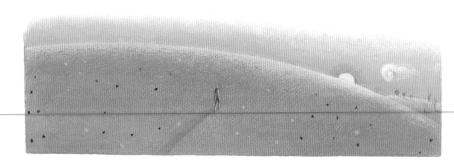

The man stopped and stared up into the heavens. What should he wish for? A falling star shot across the sky, and in that instant, the woodcutter's question was answered. He knew what he would wish for.

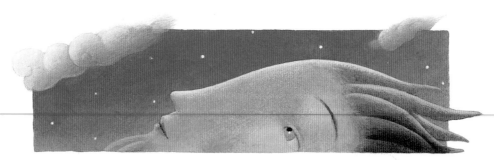

Quickly he hurried back to the cottage, and again he called his family together. The four of them gathered around the table, hardly daring to speak. The woodcutter's wife was sure her husband would ask for a baby. The old mother hoped for her sight, and the old man had his heart set on gold.

The woodcutter stood up. "I've made my decision and my wish will be this." He lifted his arm, uncurled his fingers and from his hand floated the one, single wish. Its light illuminated the dark little cottage and filled the four people with a gentle warmth.

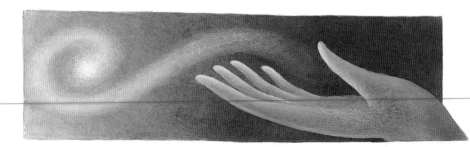

These are the words that the woodcutter spoke: "I wish that my mother could see our baby lying here in a cradle of gold."

And with that one wish, the woodcutter made everyone's wish come true.

Barefoot Books
Celebrating Art and Story

At Barefoot Books, we celebrate art and story with books that open the
hearts and minds of children from all walks of life, inspiring them to
read deeper, search further, and explore their own creative gifts.
Taking our inspiration from many different cultures, we focus on
themes that encourage independence of spirit, enthusiasm for learning,
and acceptance of other traditions. Thoughtfully prepared by writers,
artists, and storytellers from all over the world, our products combine
the best of the present with the best of the past to educate our
children as the caretakers of tomorrow.

www.barefootbooks.com